THE DAMCHARA MYSTERY

Mrinmoy Majumder

CONTENTS

Chapter 1: Preamble 1

Chapter 2: The Beginning...3

Chapter 3: The Mystery Unveiled 8

Chapter 4: The Journey 12

Chapter 5: The Meeting 16

Chapter 6: 22nd August 2020: The Day of Journey 21

Chapter 7: 24th August 2020: The Day of Discovery 33

Chapter 8: The Final Revelation 39

CHAPTER 1
PREAMBLE

Mr. Rahul Ghose, Mr. Raj Roy, and Dr. Madhusudan Gomez have been friends since childhood. They all attended the same school and college. After completing their education, one of them started his own magazine, Ghose became a mystery novelist, and Gomez became a lecturer at a government college after acquiring his doctorate from the University of Kansas in Engineering. Although they are all from Kolkata, the City of Joy, their professions have led them to different locations. Raj Roy is in Delhi, Rahul Ghose is in Mumbai, and Madhusudan Gomez is in Damchara, Assam. Despite the distance between them, they share a common interest in historical texts and enjoy deciphering the mysteries encoded within them. All three of them can read, write, and speak in 13 major languages and 27 minor languages, as well as three ancient texts that are no longer spoken by people in the modern world.

CHAPTER 2
THE BEGINNING

Now let us begin our story. This will be the first instalment.

Dr. Gomez was sitting in his living room on a Sunday morning, reading the English newspaper while sipping on his favorite Darjeeling tea. Once he was done reading, he planned to enjoy a delicious breakfast of Puri and Alur Dam, which was prepared by his wife, Mrs. Sulata Gomez.

She had come to stay with him for a few days while her office was closed for some holidays. She had also applied for leave for a few more days, and if approved, she would be able to stay with her husband for a few more days. Dr. Gomez and Mrs. Sulata got married last year in an arranged marriage, but their love for each other had blossomed quickly. However, due to their jobs, they lived in different locations and could only meet during their holidays or if one of them took leave from work.

Mr.Gomez was just going to finish his tea when the doorbell rang for two times. Upon opening the door, he was confronted by an unfamiliar figure.

"Hello Dr.Gomez"

"Hello...you are ?"

"I am Dr.Paresh Chandra Nath from Benaras Hindu University. I work there as a Professor of Linguistics."

Since he didn't know this individual and didn't have an appointment with him, Dr. Gomez wasn't entirely confident.

He therefore felt uneasy about allowing this stranger into his quarters.

Prof. Nath appears older. He has a pretty thin moustache and is rather tall. However, he is bearless. His nose stands out the most amid his exceedingly sharp facial features.

"But why have you come to meet me. I am an Engineer and I have no relation with Linguistics"…Dr.Gomez query the Professor.

"Yes you have. I know that you are interested about ancient texts and the reason I have come here to see you relates to that."

Gomez was surprised to hear this. As the passion for unravelling mysteries from the ancient text is one of the secret that was only known to three of them.

Not even his wife knows about Gomez's passion. How could this person have known this?

Prof. Nath grinned and said, "Do not be amazed, Dr. Gomez."

"Your acquaintance Mr. Ghose has given me your address and informed me that you are the only person who can help me in solving this mystery.

You will also be delighted to know that both of your friends are coming to your place day after tomorrow for this same purpose."

"But why in my place?"..Gomez was a little irritated as he was planning for a sweet holiday with his lovely wife. But now it seems that plan will not take place as he knows his friends.

They were not coming here without any reason. Something is really important here.

"May I come in?"

"Yes, Professor...please come in and take your seat."

"Thank you."...Prof.Nath took his seat and started his story.

"The mystery pertains exclusively to Dam-chara, and that's why your friends and I will gather in your home. as you are staying here for a long time"

"What" Dr.Gomez got startled..."Tell me the entire story, Professor"

"Sure."

CHAPTER 3
THE MYSTERY UNVEILED

"Let's make the long story short".... Dr.Nath started to explain the reason for his visit to the house of Dr.Gomez.

"Do you know about Tungu Language ?"

"No"

"It is the language spoken by the Tunga Tribe. They are one of the oldest tribes in the Northeast part of India.

The earliest inhabitants of the Northeast India may have been the Austroasiatic speakers from Southeast Asia, followed by Tibeto-Burman speakers from China, and by Indo-Aryan speakers from the Gangetic Plains as well as Kra-Dai speakers from southern Yunnan and Shan State.

However, this Tunga Tribes are older than these people. They are one of the very few inhabitants who had made this place their homeland when the region was under thick cover of forest.

After the invasion of Burmese, this tribe shifted its base to Damchara in the 18th century AD and after that, they are staying there for the entire duration without any hindrance. However, in the year of 1750 AD the great Sena dynasty ordered them to shift their base to someplace else.

The tribe people vehemently disagreed and a war broke out between them, As usual, the Raja were more resourceful compared to the the tribes. But the tribesmen know their jungle very well.

Consequently, the War continued for two long years.

Suddenly this war between them stopped. Everything becomes normal. Senas returned to their homeland.

The war clouds vanish into thin air. The tribes also returned to normalcy. Everything seems to be cosy between them.

But why?

Why suddenly do they shake their hands with each other and move out from continuing the war?

Why did the Raja accept his defeat?

In the History, nothing has been mentioned.

However, the result of the two long years was:

3/4 of the tribal population was killed and 1/4th of Raja's army became casualties.

But then also it was a cease-fire from both ends?!

"It is not written in the history books so we thought may be there is something written in the local dialect.

That is why I have come here to learn the Tungu Language.

After learning, I'm confident I can uncover the real reason why they suddenly stopped the war."

"Why this reason is so important? Is there any other angle to this?"...after hearing the preamble of Dr.Nath, Dr.Gomez replied.

"No...due to my present research interest, I am trying to discover this reason. Nothing else"

"OK, Dr. Nath, I am also interested in your goal. However, let me wait for my other two friends to arrive. I will discuss with them before confirming whether I can assist you or not."

"Sure, no problem. Take your time. I'll take my leave for today. Let's meet the day after tomorrow. I think your friends will be at your house by then," Professor said as he left.

CHAPTER 4
THE JOURNEY

"Hello, Madhu Hi Boudi" (Bengali Text Meaning: Sister in Law)...Raju chipped in through the open door of Dr. Gomez's house along with Ghose, their team member.

Dr.Gomez was pleased to see both of them. He and his wife warmly welcome them and ask for Tea or Coffee. As all of them are childhood friends all three preferred the same drink,i.e., Tea.

After sipping on his tea and getting comfortable on the sofa, Raj asked Gomez if he had met Professor Nath. Mr. Raj owns a print magazine and lives in Delhi. He's a tall, slim guy with a birthmark on the left side of his forehead. Ghosh, on the other hand, is a bit bulkier and of medium height, with a beard but no moustache. He's a mystery novelist currently living in Mumbai.

"Yes"

"I had a meeting with him and he was inquiring about Tungu Language."..after answering the question of Raj he took a break and sipped the tea from his right hand.

"Yes"..now Raj responded.

"This fellow has read my article about our work in deciphering ancient text. This article was published in my magazine a few months ago. But how he found out about the news of war being stopped in one day and why he is so interested in this topic that he has by his means come here to visit Gomez, that I have no idea."

"Should we join him in his quest to uncover the reason why "war stopped within one day," or should we refuse because the path to the inner parts of Damcharra is somewhat perilous?

If he has questionable intentions, we should reconsider."

Rahul was sitting idly all this time and looking at the discussions going on between his two childhood friends, but now on hearing that Raj has no idea about the motive of Prof.Nath for focusing on unearthing the details of the war between the King's men and the Tunga Tribes, he becomes anxious.

"What if he stranded us in the middle and fled with the perks of this adventure?

If we agree to be a part of this, it will be an adventure because the road to Damcharra is full of natural beauty but also danger.

There are beautiful hills with a high probability of landslides, a picturesque forest full of snakes and tigers, and tranquil rivers that flood every year.

I think Gomez knows much more than me as he is a permanent resident of this place now."

"Let us sit with Prof.Nath all together and then finalize whether we are going or not going on the trip"...after hearing Ghose, Raju replied.

CHAPTER 5
THE MEETING

"**S**ure, ..let's schedule a meeting to finalize this."...agreed Gomez.

In the evening of the same day, a meeting took place in Gomez's drawing room. There are four participants:

Dr.Madhusudan Gomez

Mr.Raj Roy

Mr.Rahul Ghose

Prof.Paresh Chandra Nath

After having tea and snacks, they are busy discussing Professor Nath's project, which aims to uncover the true reason behind the abrupt end of the war between the Tunga Tribe and the Sen dynasty.

"But Professor we want to know why are you so serious about the reason why the war has ended abruptly? Whether it has ended in one day or multiple days it has ended, that is the point we must cherish.

But why are you interested to know the reason? And you are no historian, you are linguistic. Then ?"

Professor smiled at all three.

"I understand your query. You may think that I am here for my personal gain, in terms of my career or financial stability. However, if that were the case, I could have approached any other "ancient script decoder" who would decipher the script for a fee. But sir, I am not pursuing personal gain. I am a scholar, and I am not motivated by money, as I have plenty of it.

My passion lies in uncovering the secrets within the script. If we can understand the true secret, we can apply it in modern times. This is crucial because many countries are currently at war with their neighbours, and we need to find a way to stop these wars. But how? No one seems to have the answer."

"That is the reason why if anyone can provide us with a viable solution, we have the potential to save a substantial amount of money and human lives by swiftly ending the war, possibly within a day."

Raj was taken aback by the professor's response and was unable to believe Professor Nath's altruistic intentions. He genuinely believed that the professor meant what he said.

Turning back to his friends Raj queried about their opinion.

"Where to begin ?"...

Dr.Gomez and Ghose replied simultaneously.

Both Professor and Raj understood that all four of them were now convinced about the intention of the Professor.

"We must visit a place called Jatinga Lake Viewpoint."

"Where is it, Dr. Gomez?"

"The last book written in the Tungu language was found there by a team of foreign tourists. But after that sighting, no other information was received by any of the interested people. So we must begin our search from that place. What do you think, Raj?"

"I agree with Professor. What do you think Gomez ? Ghose ?"

"I also think so"..Ghose nodded affirmatively.

"Jatinga Lake View Point is around 6 hour's drive from Damchara Main City where we are sitting now.Jatinga is a ridgetop settlement in Assam's Dima Hasao district. It is 330 km south of Guwahati. The village is home to approximately 2,500 Khasi-Pnar people plus a few Assamese. It is well-known as the site of strange bird fatalities. It is easy to go there as the place has no terrorist activities. But the road is treacherous yet heavenly.

If we leave at dawn, we can arrive within 2 pm."..Gomez paused and looked at Prof.Nath..."Will I book a car for the four of us tomorrow?"

"Yes ...Sure" with this Prof.Nath concluded the meeting as he had to run for his lodge such that he could arrange his luggage for tomor-row's voyage to unearth the mystery of "Why does a long-term war end so suddenly?"

CHAPTER 6
22ND AUGUST 2020: THE DAY OF JOURNEY

At roughly 4 a.m., three friends board Dr. Gomez's car and drive to the lodge where Prof. Nath is staying. When they arrived at the lodge, Professor got into the car, and the four of them set out for the Jatinga Lake View Point near the Jatinga River.

After a while, the four travelers forgot their goal and became entirely lost in the grandeur of the countryside through which they were driving. Nature has bestowed all of its blessings on this place. Magnificent hills, a profound forest, and an idyllic road cut across this heavenly environment.

Ultimately around 10 am they reach Jatinga Lake View Point. Now their original work will start. First, they have to find the place where the foreigners have found the manuscript written in the Tunga Language. As per the information collected by the Professor, it was a tea shop where the foreigners had found the manuscript. But there are two to three teashops in this place and none of them has any idea about this. By showing the pictures of that group of foreigners, no one was able to identify them, let alone locate the manuscript.

After investigating the other shops also they could not find any whereabouts of the manuscript. All four were dejected and decided to call it quits for the day. They booked two rooms in a homestay just a kilometre away from Lake View Point.

The homestay is situated in a charming village surrounded by lush greenery and inhabited by a small, close-knit community. The village has only one grocery store and a handful of tea shops that cater to the daily needs of its residents. The homestay itself boasts six spacious rooms, all of which are positioned around a serene Buddhist temple.

The owner of the house and his family make it a daily ritual to visit the temple at both dawn and dusk to pay their respects to their family deity. The proprietor, an octogenarian, lives with his wife and two adult daughters. His wife is approximately 70 years old, and both daughters have transitioned from their adolescent years into young adulthood.

The homestay is peaceful and well-organized. After the daylong journey, none of the four wasted any time. They freshened up, had dinner, and withdrew to their cosy beds. Raj and Rahul are staying in one room, and Dr. Gomez and Prof. Nath are in the other. Both rooms are located side by side.

The next morning, Raj, Rahul, Madhusudan, and Prof. Nath were having tea at a nearby shop. They felt refreshed and ready to begin their search. After paying the bill for the tea and a few biscuits, they started to survey the area, discussed with local people, and also looked in the government offices located there. They also visited the old temples and libraries in the area. However, all their searches were in vain. No manuscripts written in the Tungu language were found, and most of the people didn't know about the Tunga Tribe either.

So with a dejected heart and frustrated face they returned to their homestay. All four of them were discussing with each other about their next steps at Raj and Rahul's room when the owner of the homestay knocked.

"I heard that you four are looking for a manuscript written in Tungu Script"...he queried.

The owner of the homestay is quite fit even if his age is eighty-one. Although all his hair colour has now turned white and so has his moustache and beard but his voice, walking style and attitude still resemble a jovial youth.

"I heard you are looking for a manuscript written in Tungu Script. But I am sorry to say that you will not find that here. No one from the tribe now lives here. Only few people who are direct descendants of the tribe can be found at the village located at 3 km across the deep forest.

But the tribe people are extremely friendly and they will welcome you warmly. But still I doubt whether they have the manuscript or not because all of them now speak and write in English. They are educated by the Christian Missionaries.

So I dont think there are anyone who now speaks or write in the Tungu language.But still you can give it a try."..saying this he takes farewell from the four members of the team who have come here in search of the manu-script written in Tungu language.

"Thank you so much"...Raj told the owner of the homestay gleefully."You have saved a lot of time and cost. We will surely give it a try"

Accordingly, the four members started their journey towards the remotest village of the place. While going through the jungles they were wondering how the roads are constructed here and that also so accurately. As the place is totally inaccessible if these roads are not constructed. They all are thanking the engineers and planners of the road that is taking them towards their destiny.

Although the road does not lead to the exact location of the village. After a while the team understood that. Fortunately, few people of the village were returning back to their homes and they are from that village only. They requested them to park their car on the road and walk with them towards the village. Accordingly, all the four members start to follow the group of people and ultimately reach the village.

As told to them by the owner of the homestay, villagers welcome the team with open hearts and offer them refreshments. However, their search for the manuscript remains inconclusive. As no one from the village even read in the Tungu language. They said that the last person to know this language died last year in a landslide which also destroyed his house and other belongings. His family built a new house nearby but all his possessions are now lost in the oblivion. Now everybody of us can write and speak in English or Hindi or Assamese but not in the Tungu Language.

Although the four members of the team were highly impressed by the way these remote villagers were communicating with them in clear English but they also understood that it is now nearly impossible to find a manuscript written in that ancient script. So they decided to quit and return to their homestay. They also decided that they would return today to Damcharra.

Accordingly, they thanked the villagers and drove straight to the homestay. There they inform the owner about their encounter with the villagers. Then they check out from the homestay. Before going out from Jatinga they stopped their car into one of the tea shops they had not visited earlier. It is located just beside the highway which brings them here.

They ordered Tea and biscuits. While sipping the tea Raj was suddenly distracted by a sound and looked behind him. The tea shop has a rectangular floor shape. On one side the reception is placed from where the tea and snacks are distributed. All the other side benches were arranged for the customers. Raj and Rahul were seated just opposite the reception. Prof.Nath and Dr.Gomez were sitting in the benches placed at the left-hand wall.

While looking behind Raj noticed a framed artwork. By looking at a distance it can be understood that it is at least 50 years old. The artwork was a war scene where two parties are looking at something with all their weapon in hand. One party seems to be a part of the King's soldier and the other party is dressed in tribal attire. Raj got curious and informed Rahul about this. Rahul also looks behind and as he can not see the picture clearly he asks a staff of the tea shop to bring the picture to him.

On seeing this Gomez and Prof.Nath also come near to that place and all of them start to inspect the picture. But they are doing so in a shabby manner as they know that their quest has failed and they have lots of time in hand. But after carefully observing the picture all four of them have the same question.

"Where are the two parties at war looking at?"

They are not looking at each other as they should be when two parties are at war. Now by observing their dress and weapons, it can be easily understood that they are at war and this war is taking place in ancient times which can be at the time when the mighty Ahom Dynasty ruled this area or may be older than that.

But where are they looking at?

They are looking at a person standing on the highland. This person has a rod in his hand which has a symmetric shape"...Gomez whispered to the team.

"But that is impossible because the attire and weapon of the army at war indicate that this picture is drawn at a time when weapons can not be made in a symmetric shape."

"Ancient civilizations used materials available to them, like wood, stone, fire, and metal, to make weapons. Here's how weapons were made in different eras:

Stone Age

Weapons were made from stone and wood, shaped and joined together. For example, a hand axe was made by shaping a stone into a cutting edge and attaching it to a wooden handle using animal tendons or sinew.

Early humans

Spears were first made from bamboo as early as the 9th or 10th century.

Mesopotamia

By the middle of the 3rd millennium BC, mace heads were cast from copper.

Bronze Age

Weapons were made from bronze, which was harder and more durable than copper. Bronze was produced by alloying copper with tin or arsenic.

Later civilizations

Weapons were made from iron and steel.

Early people used weapons for hunting food and protection. Ancient civilizations developed specialized bows and arrows, spears, and swords for warfare. Some civilizations also used "liquid fire", which was projected onto enemy ships using siphons and could burn on water."..Gomez continued.

"But the rod this person is carrying and if I am not wrong it is made in the modern era. Another point to observe is the attire of this person. It is quite modern compared to the clothing worn by the kings men and the tribes."...explained Prof.Nath.

On consultation with the staff and also with the owner of the shop who is quite old they learned that this artwork was gifted by a librarian working near their village.

"Which village?"

.. shouted Prof. Nath in excitement.

"…..the village where the Tungu Tribes stay" the owner replied with a frightened tone. He was a little shaky due to the increased tone of Professor.

"That means the village we had visited."...Raj added.

"Let us go to the village again. This may be our last chance."

..Prof.Nath concluded and ran towards their car.

CHAPTER 7
24TH AUGUST 2020: THE DAY OF DISCOVERY

The four individuals searching for the manuscript written in the Tungu language have returned to the village where the descendants of the Tunga Tribe reside.

Upon arriving, they inquire with the villagers about the library that the tea shop owner mentioned.

Initially, the villagers were confused about which library was being referred to.

However, an elderly person provided them with directions to the library and mentioned that very few people visit it nowadays. As a result, most of the recently grown-up villagers are unaware of its existence.

According to the guidance of that person the four person reach the library. However, the present librarian told them that he don't know about any such manuscript or artwork. But he also added that if they visit the home of the former librarian then he can help. His house is also in this village.

So our searching team run towards the house of the former librarian and found him sitting in the verandah and sipping his evening tea.His age can be understood from the signs in his face and his white hair. He is thin and wear spectacles. By looking at him one can conclude that he is a very methodical person.

"Welcome to my home. How can I help you? You are not from my village. From where have you came and why ?"...he queried.

"We all have come to you to ask you about this artwork,"..Raj showed him the picture of the artwork he had taken from the tea shop. "The shop owner told us that you can enlighten about this picture and also about a manuscript written in Tungu Script."

"Sorry".. "I cant help you in this regard.I have never seen any such artwork. But yes I have heard about this Tungu Script and about that war which has been stopped in one day.

But I don't know about any such manuscript which is written in that language."

Prof.Nath and all three friends were frustrated as their last source of that manuscript had also failed them.

"If you could have helped us we can complete our research and our findings can forward our knowledge about the wartime strategy to finish war within a very short time.It could have saved a lot of money and lives also."..Prof.Nath explained to the old librarian.

"OK,let me think about it for a little more time. Come inside my room and have a seat. Sorry for making you stand so long. I stay here alone. My daughter stay abroad. I am not anyone from the Tungu Tribe. I come here as a Senior Librarian and then retired. After retiring I found that instead of going to a city like Guwahati or Silchor it is better to stay here for the rest of my life. This is a beautiful place to stay.You will be surprised to know that I am 90 and totally fit and fine. This is only because of this area,its water and air ,the villagers all are extremely pure and pious."

"My daughter is a Professor at a College in London. She is passionate about her research. Seeing the quest for knowledge in your eyes I remembered my daughter. That is why I will help you all. Let me search my collection of old books."

The nonagenarian slowly stood up and walked inside his house. After two long hours, he comes back. He is drenched in his sweat. He has dirt all over his shirt and dhoti that he was wearing at that time. But the good thing is he has something in his hand.

"Here is your manuscript. The last text where the Tungu Script was used. Turn to the last page. You will find the artwork whose picture you have shown me."...the old librarian with shaking hand and breathing heavily hand the manuscript to the hand of the Prof.Nath.

"Are you okay? Please sit and take rest. Thank you so much for your help. You don't know how much you have helped us," said Prof. Nath with an enlightened face and excited voice as he repeatedly thanked the nonagenarian, as did the other four friends.

It was quite late. So the old librarian requests them to stay here for the day. At that time they also remembered that they have already checked out from the home stay. So they accept his invitation.

After dinner, the old librarian and all four of them sat and discussed the manuscript.

The elderly librarian was also assisting them in decoding the language.

The most typical method is to compare an ancient language to known languages to find parallels in grammar, lexicon, and syntax. So, if researchers are familiar with Latin and Ancient Greek, they can utilize their knowledge to interpret documents from civilizations that were neighbours of the Greeks and Romans.

The three friends, who are experts in this field, attempted to apply various methods such as Letter Coding and Semantics to decipher the language from the manuscripts.

But everything yielded nothing.

That night, they all worked until 4 am. At the old librarian's request, they went to their rooms and called it a night. As a result, they all woke up late the next morning. After enjoying a cup of tea, all four of them thanked the old librarian once more and hopped into their car to head back to Damchara.

CHAPTER 8
THE FINAL REVELATION

In Damchara also all four of them worked continuously with the manuscripts but they could not decipher the script.

"Impossible…I resign"…frustrated Raj gave up.

"So am I"…Rahul seconded him.

"Same here, my friend. This is the first time we have failed to decrypt an ancient text. Sorry, Prof. Nath. I think you need to consult other experts in the field. Maybe they can help," Gomez concluded, noting the emotions of his friend.

"Don't be disheartened, all of you. Failure is the mother of success. We fail to know that we will find success. Don't worry, let us have tea from your wife. She makes good tea," Prof. Nath tried to encourage them. But all three friends were extremely disappointed with their failure.

"It has been a week since we started working on this script. Our vacation is coming to an end and we need to return to our workplace. How much more time will we waste?" ...Raj questioned Prof. Nath after taking a sip of tea.

"Same here, Raj. I need to start my new novel. But how much longer can we procrastinate? The publisher keeps urging me to begin writing.". .Rahul also joined the chorus.

"I have to begin my class. The new session is going to start tomorrow."..

Rahul put down is empty tea glass on the tray and stood up to go to the toilet. At that time Moumita come to collect all the empty tea glasses. Ray of sunlight was coming through the window of the drawing room. The tray with the tea glasses was kept just beside the manuscript.

The sunlight after refraction through the tea glasses falls on the manuscript.

At that time Moumita observed that the cover page of the manuscript is written in Hindi. So she casually communicated to all that why they are so confused with the script. It is simple Hindi.

"Don't you know Hindi script?"..Moumita shouted at them in a friendly tone.

"This is Hindi. And all four of you have been working day and night for the last seven days and can not read Hindi? How surprising ?"..with a giggle on her face Moumita took the tray with the tea glass and tried to leave the room. But all the four men stopped her.

"What are you saying ?"

"Are we all idiots? We all know how to read Hindi."..Dr. Gomez angrily replied to his wife.

"Yes Boudi we all know Hindi. I stay in Delhi where Hindi is the only language of communication"...Raj supported his friend.

Now Gomez took the book and observed the cover page.

"Here look at it now."

Moumita was dumbfounded.

"Arre..yes it is not Hindi..it is something else. But put it on the table. It will be Hindi.

I think that is the trick those ancient fellows have developed. "...surprised at the sudden conversion of the text to an unknown script Moumita tried to defend herself.

Accordingly, Dr. Gomez placed the manuscript on the table. The cover page displayed the same unknown script referred to as Tungu.

Dr.Gomez was just going to make fun of his wife at that moment something struck his mind.

"Wait"..."put the tray with the glass also"... "In the same way it was initially arranged"

"OK".. "Here you go"...Moumita arranged the tray in the same manner it was their initially. The sun light falls on the manuscript through the glass.

Now each of the members see the place where the lights are falling on the manuscript. Yes the script in that area has turned to hindi.

"It is not hindi.

It is Devnagari"..corrected Raj with a whispering voice.

The four members except Moumita was astonished and surprised with the technology adopted by those ancient tribe men. Except Moumita.,she left the room with a winning smile.

"So this is the trick. They have written the manuscript in such a manner that the script will only decipher into Devnagari when light is diffracted and reflected from the manuscript.

But whether this property of light was invented at that time ?"..Dr.Gomez asked every other person of the room.

"No..not at that time"..replied Prof.Nath. He was shocked by the entire proceedings of the last two hours. He has not predicted that the mystery will be solved in such a manner.

"So friends now let us finish reading the manuscript to know the reason or have an idea about the cause of the abrupt end of the war."...with a mixed emotions Prof.Nath regroup the members and tried to organize them to sort the main problem.

After reading the manuscript by dividing the manuscript into four parts with the help of tea glasses, it was revealed that the man in the picture who was wearing a modern dress and carrying a rod; made up of some modern materials; came to the village roaming through the forest where the tribes were hiding.

Seeing the plight of the tribe he shared 10 such rods with selected tribesmen.

Then the next morning, all the weapons carried by the king's men broke when they touched the rod being carried by the 10 tribe men and their mysterious saviour.

Seeing this the Senapati of the kingmen understood that they could not win the war if the tribesmen had that rod. So he thought it was better to make friends and steal the technology from the tribes. However, the war ends, but no trace of the technology, rod, or saviour can be found. It seemed that he had vanished into thin air.

With this, the manuscript concluded that he was treated as a godmen by the tribes at the time the manuscript was written.

"Fortunately, this manuscript was written on that war only. But we will never know who that person was. Whether he is a time traveler? "..Rahul asked with a puzzled tone.

"God knows. But at least the mystery of the war is revealed. That is enough for me."

As soon as the professor finished speaking, he stood up, bid farewell to everyone, and left the room. After he departed, the three friends discussed the revelation among themselves, feeling relieved and happy that their hard work had paid off and their reputation had not been compromised.

Suddenly, they realized that Professor Nath had forgotten his spectacle case. Rahul went to the door to look for him, but he was nowhere to be found.

Raj and Madhusudan joined in the search, but there was no trace of the professor. They even went outside the house, but the roads were empty and the professor had vanished into thin air. It seemed impossible that an old man could disappear so quickly.

"Hey Raj you must have his phone number of him?"…Gomez asked Raj.

"Yes..let me dial him"...Raj replied. But on dialing multiple times also the phone is out of reach.

"Nevermind. Find his office address on the website. We will post the case to him. He may also contact us if this case is important to him."...explained Rahul.

But on searching the internet and calling his University it was found that there is no Prof.Nath who worked at that University.

Then??? Who is Prof.Nath? Why has he come to them?

Gomez, feeling agitated, instructed his friends to open the case so that he could see its contents, finding the situation to be humiliating.

On opening the case they found a diamond which can be sold in the market for lakhs of rupees. Under this diamond was a note.

All of them quickly unfurl the note.

"Your Remuneration. Thank you for uncovering the secret of my clan. The man who shared the rod with the tribes is my uncle. He knows how to travel through time. However, this invention of his was not recognized by anyone, not even by our family.

As a result, he was ostracized and thrown out of our clan due to blasphemy. But I believed in him. I apologize for giving you a false identity of myself. Please keep my identity a secret for the betterment of human civilization. If powerful people discover this technology, the consequences could be severe. Once again, thank you for everything, especially the tea from Moumita.

Bless you all."

*This story was originally published
in ITell Newsletter*